WORST JOB EVER

Worst Ever Series - Book 4

J Frank Sander

ISBN-13: 9798807646989
ISBN-10: 1477123456

Cover design by: Art Painter
Library of Congress Control Number: 2018675309
Printed in the United States of America

PROLOGUE

After I dropped out of two different colleges, my father told me that I needed to get a "real education". He thought that if an academic education hadn't taken hold, a dose of education from the school of hard knocks would provide me with the teachable moments that I needed to become a mature and productive adult.

My father also figured that experience as a laborer in a factory might be the motivation that I needed to return to college for a degree. So, since he was the director of personnel at a large manufacturing company, he arranged for me to be hired as a forklift operator in the company's drop-forge.

CHAPTER 1 - WEEK 1

I was introduced to an electric forklift and told how the controls work during the third shift in a huge building. The shift ran from 11 PM to 7 AM. The forklift had a steering wheel like a car, a throttle pedal, a brake pedal, a forward and reverse lever on the steering column, and a lever that was mounted on what you might call a dashboard to lift and lower the split forks. Another lever tilted the fork tips up and down. I had to climb up into the seat which was about four feet off the floor. The only instrument on the dashboard was a gauge that indicated the amount of electric power the machine had. There were a couple of lights that I assumed were indicators of something, but I never learned what they were for.

"This baby will lift about a ton," said the third shift trucking foreman who was training me. "Any more than that, and the rear wheels come off the ground. You don't want that to happen because you got the front-wheel-drive and rear-wheel steering. You won't be able to control where she goes. If you need anything heavier than a ton lifted, you gotta call for one of the two-ton forklifts or a crane."

"I can do that," I said with a yawn, regretting that I hadn't downed a couple more cups of coffee before heading over to the factory that night. I foolishly had not slept since morning, wanting to get a day full of fun in before starting my new job.

"You'll be on third shift for about two weeks before you go on first shift in the drop forge," the foreman told me. "So what I want you to do is, drive this rig around the steel stores all night, and move stuff around."

The steel stores department was about the size of an airport hangar. Huge steel racks stood ten feet high, supporting heavy-duty shelves in long rows the length of the building. The shelves held steel bins loaded with various-sized forgings.

The foreman continued, "Get used to picking these full bins up and putting them where they need to be. They're heavy, so don't drop 'em. Some will go in a designated area on the floor, and others will go on the shelf racks in these aisles. Each bin has a code number on it. Match the number on the bin to the one on the shelf and put it there."

"I can do that," I said.

The foreman looked me up and down, taking in my street clothes and sneakers.

"You need to wear steel-toe shoes, a helmet, safety glasses, earplugs, and gloves in the forge. You can get the plugs and safety glasses from the nurses' station. I have a spare helmet and glasses that you can use for a couple of days, but you'll need to have all your gear before the end of this week.

"You'll also want to wear long sleeves and some kind of face protection, like a bandana. Since it's cool in here, you can forget the gloves and bandana. But you're gonna want them in the forge. It's hot and smoky in there. Now get up on that seat and try to drive this thing."

"Oh, and by the way," he added, "the rig has rear-wheel steering, so it's different from a car."

Once seated I had a large two-way radio on my right, which meant that I always had to climb onto and off of the seat on the left side. There was a steel mesh canopy over my head. Behind me was a huge battery that needed to be replaced after every shift. The battery was so big and heavy that it had to be removed and re-placed with a crane that was operated by a hand-held control box.

I shifted the forklift into 'forward' and started down an empty aisle that was wide enough to turn around and go in the opposite direction. That is, it would have been if the forklift had front-wheel steering. But when I tried to turn, the rear end swung around, pivoting, and striking hard against a rack loaded with bins full of stuff. Fortunately, the rack was bolted to the floor or I would have caused a domino effect that would have brought the entire building down.

"Hey, Dumbass," the trainer shouted from the end of the aisle, "I told yuh 'rear-wheel steering'! Watch where you're going!"

I drove the forklift up to him, apologized, and told him that I hoped that I didn't cause any damage to the rack.

He shook his head and then chuckled. "It happens to everyone. Keep practicing and I'll check on you later." With that, he left me alone.

It didn't take me long to get into the hang of steering with the rear wheels. It took a little longer for me to learn to judge distances. But by the end of the shift, I could center the six-foot forks under a bin, tilt the forks upward while lifting, and then drive with a four-foot-high bin loaded onto the forks without hitting anything.

But the most frightening part was lifting a bin of stuff and placing it on any shelf that was higher than eye level. The highest shelves were ten feet off the floor. Neglecting to tilt the forks downward while backing away from a shelf would pull that heavy bin off and cause it to drop onto the steel mesh canopy over my head from five feet above. The first time I did it I was sure that I was going to die.

But I didn't die. Instead, I learned how to drive the forklift without hitting anything. I even was able to place bins on the highest shelves without incident.

I sat proudly behind the wheel and navigated expertly between the racks, lifting bins, and placing them on the highest racks with finesse. In my mind, I saw my future. Who needs a college education? I imagined that I would learn to operate every piece of equipment in the factory. People would rely on my expertise to increase production efficiency. I saw myself becoming a foreman in the trucking department, perhaps a plant supervisor. And someday I might even purchase the plant and become a multi-millionaire.

CHAPTER 2 - WEEK 3

I didn't sleep at all the night before I was supposed to start working in the forge on the first shift. I had been on third shift for two weeks and my body was now used to being awake during the night hours, so I tossed and turned all night long. I was a little groggy when I punched the time clock at ten to seven in the morning. I walked down the aisle toward the staging area for the drop-forge forklifts. My steel-toe shoes looked like something that would be worn by the Frankenstein monster and felt like they weighed about ten pounds each. I was dressed in jeans, a long-sleeved undershirt under a denim work shirt, my helmet, and my safety glasses. A red bandana was tied loosely around my neck and my earplugs were snug in my ears.

I arrived in the staging area and climbed into the seat of a forklift, switched the radio on to inform the trucking department dispatcher that I was ready to start my shift, and then turned the key. Nothing happened. I turned the key off and on again and again and again until the attendant helpfully called out, "Hey, Genius. It ain't gonna go without a battery."

He pointed with both hands like someone guiding a jet onto the runway. I turned my eye in the direction he was pointing and saw that the battery was still attached to a chain and suspended above the forklift from the crane.

The battery was covered by a heavy hinged steel lid that, when raised, revealed a large open battery compartment. I jumped off the forklift and waited until the battery was in place. I put my hand on the lid, intending to hurry the process along as the attendant had reached across the battery to unhook the lift chain.

Without permission, I started to lower the lid, which weighed far more than I had anticipated. It slipped out of my hand and slammed down on the attendance's arm. He howled in pain and screamed, "You idiot! You broke my arm!" I lifted the lid with effort and he ran off toward the first aid station.

I looked around. There were no other attendants nearby, the lights on the forklift dash were glowing and the radio buzzing, so I shrugged to myself, climbed onto the seat, and drove away.

I called dispatch and said, "Sorry for the delay. Battery change."

The radio crackled and the dispatcher said, "You'll be tending drop hammers number one through nine. You better get down there right away. The hammer crews are waiting for you."

It was my first official day in the drop forge and I proudly drove my forklift straight into hell.

CHAPTER 3 – THE FORGE

Nine drop hammers were lined up along one wall. There was a low furnace between each hammer, hot enough to turn steel red hot and malleable. Each hammer had a crew of five men: a hammerman who ran the crew, an assistant hammerman, a lubricator who swabbed grease on the hammer components and dies, a scale blower, who used a high-pressure air hose to blow impurities off the pieces that were to be pounded into shape, and a furnace loader.

I noticed that every hammer had a large steel shield in front of it. The shield was on rollers so that it could be pushed aside during die exchanges. I asked one of the scale blowers what the shields were for.

The scale blower, whose name was Floyd, said, "Those screens are there to keep pieces from flying into the main aisle. You see, I blow scale from the backside, and the junk comes out the front. Yuh don't wanna get hit by the junk because it's hot as blazes."

"I bet that would hurt," I said.

"That's not even the worst of it. Sometimes the hammermen screw up. That hammer can come down and strike a red hot billet wrong and squirt the piece out the front side like a red hot bullet."

On the opposite side of the main aisle were more furnaces containing the die sets needed for shaping the billet pieces to be manufactured. The die sets came with a top and a bottom half that had to be heated to eight hundred degrees. The dies were slippery, so to keep them together, strips of emery cloth were placed between the top and bottom halves. Otherwise, they might slide apart, with the top die dropping to the floor off the forklift forks. The emery cloth provided friction to keep that from happening.

Each set of dies had a number scrawled on the outside with chalk. That number matched the number of the job that was to be performed. I was responsible for pulling the dies out of the furnace and delivering them to the correct hammer.

The forge was not well lit, but in the distance, I saw a furnace tender waving at me. I pulled alongside and looked down at him. He stepped onto my truck and put his lips close to my ear.

"We gotta get some of these dies onto the hammers. Some are already there because third shift crews got them ready before they left. Every crew gets paid according to the number of pieces that they make, and extra pay for setup."

Then he walked down the aisle and opened every furnace door to read the die number until he found the one that he needed with me following slowly behind. The correct die set was finally identified, so he opened the furnace doors wide and waved me forward. I slid the forks under the bottom die, tilted them back, put my truck in reverse, and pulled it out. Then the laborer ran ahead of me until we reached the hammer where the crew was waiting for me. The process was painfully slow.

In my mind. I saw myself as the plant supervisor. I'd solve the problem, making the die selection process easier by writing the die number on a slate board on the outside of each furnace so that the furnace attendant wouldn't have to hunt for the correct die set. I imagined myself getting a huge cash bonus for increasing plant efficiency.

CHAPTER 4 - WEEK 6

Although the windows along the west wall were always open, the air in the plant was still hot and oppressive. The forge was dirty and noisy. Even with ear protection, I was beginning to have symptoms of tinnitus. My ears kept ringing long after my shift ended.

Besides delivering dies to the hammers in my area, another part of my job was to supply the furnaces that were positioned next to the hammers with steel billets. A billet is a hunk of metal that is rectangular, circular, or square. It is heated until it reaches the elasticity required to pound it into shape. I was told that most of the furnaces burned at about fifteen hundred degrees; some much hotter, depending on what kind of steel the billet was made from.

Here is where the bandana came in handy. I made sure to pull the bandana up over my nose and mouth before carrying a bin full of billets over to a furnace. Then I drove the forklift as far as possible into the furnace until I could no longer stand the intense heat, set the bin down, and used the forks to turn the bin over. After I tipped the bin over, I'd tip it back upright and remove the empty bin.

A furnace loader operated a conveyor system that advanced the billet into the furnace depths. The hammerman's assistant pulled the glowing billet out of the other end of the furnace with a pair of tongs and positioned it on the die for shaping.

The first day after my shift I went home and looked in the mirror and saw that I had singed eyebrows.

One day I carried a loaded bin to one of the furnaces, but the crew was on a short break, and I had a chance to talk to the furnace loader that worked with the hammer crew. His name was Tommy and he was close to fifty years old. I asked him how long he'd been working at the company.

"Twenty-seven years," Tommy said, looking down into his coffee cup. "I was just out of high school and signed on temporarily until I had a little money saved so I could maybe go back to school. But I hated working here and decided to quit after a month."

"That was twenty-seven years ago?" I asked.

He took a drink from his coffee cup and looked up at me with sad eyes. "I was gonna quit. I was. I had made up my mind. But then I learned that the company gives employees a turkey for Thanksgiving and pays a nice bonus at Christmas time. I like turkey, and I needed the extra pay, so I decided to work until just after Christmas."

"You never went back to school?" I asked.

Tommy reflected for a while. Then he shook his head sadly and said, "I was gonna quit that January, but then I realized that the company gives two weeks of paid vacation after a year. So I thought that I would stick it out until I got my vacation pay."

He put down his coffee cup and lit a cigarette. "You don't want to do what I did, Kid," he said, those sad eyes holding my attention. "After I got my vacation pay, I remembered that I had another turkey and a bonus coming in a few months, so I stayed on for that."

I don't understand," I said. "Twenty-seven years on a job that you hate?"

Tommy shrugged. "It's been twenty-seven years working from vacation to bonus to vacation to the bonus."

The break was over and Tommy went back to work, but not before he said, "Don't be me, Kid."

My imagination took me into the future. I was arriving at home after my shift, my face covered with soot and grease, my eyebrows singed, my clothes filthy. I hugged my kids and told my wife, "Only ten more years, and I can retire," and went straight to bed.

CHAPTER 5 - WEEK 15

Floyd, the scale blower on hammer nine, and I had become friends. We sat and talked during just about every break. I learned that he'd been working in the forge for close to thirty-five years. He had a family, a dog that he loved and bragged about often, and he had earned a black belt in karate. He was a wiry guy, five feet seven inches tall with a bald head. He moved like a martial art fighter, always light on the balls of his feet and full of calm energy.

One day he told me, "I've been thinking about you."

"You have?" I asked. "What were you thinking?"

"Look, you're a nice kid, you have a good head on your shoulders, even if you're not a very good forklift driver."

It was true. I wasn't anywhere near as good as any of the other forklift drivers in the forge. I ran over a guy's foot once, dropped dies more than once, and backed into a laborer and put him out of work for two weeks.

Floyd said, "You need to get out of this place as soon as you can. Don't be like me or any of these other guys." Then he pointed down the aisle, "Yuh see that guy over there? How old do you think he is?"

I looked toward a man walking as if in slow motion. His back was bent and his head lowered so that he was looking at the floor when he walked. His arms hung motionless at his sides and he shuffled his feet. I had the impression that he was in serious pain.

"I don't know," I said. "Seventy?"

Floyd smiled. "I know that guy. He's fifty-nine years old. Came to work here when he was eighteen. This place can suck the life out of you, Kid. Do me a favor and get the hell out of here before it's too late. Tell you what. I have a Cadillac that you can own if you leave this place while you can."

My mind took me thirty-six years into my future. I pictured myself walking down the aisle toward the time clock at the end of my shift, my feet shuffling like a homeless person, my body exhausted, my back bent and aching, and my head pounding. I imagined myself raising my hand to punch the clock, so tired that I could barely lift my arm to insert my card into the slot.

CHAPTER 6 - WEEK 37

It was near the end of my shift and the crew on hammer 9 had just finished a job. They'd be clocking out at exactly three. But they had a little time left, so they decided to do a die change for the second shift crew so to receive the extra pay.

The job required two different sets of dies. The first set was a flat die. Both the top and bottom halves were perfectly flat to pound the billet into a thick round pancake shape, like a large hockey puck. Then after shaping the billet, a second die set would be installed to pound the piece into its final shape.

The hammers in this forge were powered by steam. Each hammer had a steam chamber above and an anvil below. A heavy ram hangs above the anvil, attached to a heavy steel rod. A two-way valve is engaged to fill the steam chamber, and a thick bushing, called a gland, holds the steam at bay until the hammerman wants the ram to drop.

The hammerman uses steel tongs to hold the red hot billet in place and turn it if needed. He steps on a treadle to release the ram which pounds the billet into the die's shape with the force of the built-up steam. When he steps off the treadle, the ram lifts, ready to drop with thousands of pounds of force every time he steps on the treadle.

During a die change, the steam valve is closed and the ram is propped with a two-by-four so that it cannot accidentally fall while the dies are being changed. Then the dies are placed on the anvil by the forklift driver. The bottom half of the die is locked into place. The top half of the die is manually aligned, then the ram is manually lowered and the top half is also locked into place. Bad alignment could cause the billet to squirt out of either the front or the back of the hammer on a hard ram strike.

The hammerman wears a thick leather apron for protection in case of a billet squirting out the back. The steel curtain keeps an errant billet from squirting out into the main aisle.

I was nearby when one of the larger hammers was having trouble. For some reason the large billet, weighing close to a hundred pounds and being shaped by the hammerman, kept moving out of position. He told the crew to shut the hammer down until they could figure out why that was happening.

But the foreman walked over and insisted that he make another piece so that he could observe what the hammer might have been doing to cause the problem. He stood off to the side as the glowing billet was placed on the die.

The hammerman stepped on the treadle and the hot piece flew out the back of the hammer, hit the hammerman in the groin like a cannon shot, and flung him backward fifteen feet into a large floor fan that tipped over and fell on him.

If he hadn't been wearing the apron he might have been killed. Nevertheless, the hammerman suffered a broken hip, a concussion, a broken eye socket, and a ruptured spleen. He was carried out on a stretcher.

CHAPTER 7 - END OF SHIFT

It was twenty-five minutes before the end of the first shift. The crew on hammer nine wanted to do a quick set-up to gain the extra pay. My radio squawked and the dispatcher's voice came through. "Go to hammer nine for a die change."

Changing dies is relatively easy and safe when proper procedures are followed. I had done it hundreds of times without incident.

I approached hammer nine where the crew was waving franticly at me. When I arrived, they directed me to a die-furnace that was located halfway down the aisle from the hammer. The furnace door was already open, a flat die heated and ready to be removed. The furnace tender told me to carry the die to hammer nine.

I put my forks under the die and as I pulled away from the furnace, I saw the top half shift a little. I immediately realized that someone had neglected to put the emery cloth between the top and bottom halves.

I should have refused to move the die set, but the hammer crew was anxious to get the setup done and I wanted them to earn the extra setup pay. So I drove my forklift to the hammer carefully, making sure that the two halves stayed together. I kept my eye on the die set as I went and saw the top half shifting and sliding as I went.

I pulled up to the front of the hammer and waited for the crew to get ready to install the die and lock it to the anvil and ram.

I voiced my concern. "These dies are shifting all over the place. Don't know if this is a good idea."

I should have refused to lift the die set outright. The die's slippery top half had turned about 25 degrees as it sat on the bottom half.

So I hesitated. But the crew was impatient. They were running out of time and needed to get the setup done before three o'clock. They had about ten minutes to get it done or they would not receive the extra pay. The hammerman demanded that I proceed.

I reluctantly tilted the fork tips up, lifted the complete set of dies to the correct height, slowly pulled my forklift forward to the correct position, and lowered the die set toward the anvil. Again I hesitated to tilt the forks downward.

The hammerman walked up to me and said, "What are you waiting for? Just tilt the forks down and pull out fast. The dies should just drop into place."

"The top die is crooked. It slid on the trip over," I said.

The hammerman looked at the die set and said, "I'll line the top up after you drop it."

"I can put them up above the anvil while still on the forks, and you can lock the top half before I drop the bottom," I said.

The hammerman looked at his watch. "No time. Drop them now."

I did as I was told.

I tilted the forks downward slightly and put the forklift into reverse. I hit the throttle and started to pull out fast. Without warning the top half of the die slid off the bottom half and fell toward the backside of the hammer.

Suddenly the ram made a full-force strike under a full head of steam as the crew fled in every direction, climbing onto the furnace walls, running toward the open windows, and into the main aisle. The ram struck my forks, and I was thrown upward, my helmeted head hitting the steel canopy. An instant later I was hit with hot steam blowing down on me from above. It sounded like a hurricane. I instinctively covered my face, the steam burning the exposed flesh between my gloves and my long-sleeved shirt.

Hot steam blew across the main aisle at the front of the hammer, so one of the crew members who had found safety in the aisle ran over to my truck and closed the steel safety curtain around my forklift, trapping me inside of what felt like a pressure cooker.

The radio on my right kept me from leaping off to the forklift on the right side. And a floor-to-ceiling pillar on my left prevented me from jumping off to the left side.

I managed to escape by throwing my body onto the battery cover behind my seat, rolling off, and dropping to the concrete floor. Then I crawled on my belly under the safety screen.

I sat on the floor with my back against the screen, shaking uncontrollably, my heart racing, and breathing hard, when one of the crew walked up to me, face red with anger. He didn't ask me if I was alright. Instead, he screamed at me.

"You idiot! You almost killed our crew!"

My mind raced. I saw myself in the future, my face burned to a crisp, scars that made me look like a movie monster, my arm broken, and my eardrums punctured. In my imagination, I had to go through months of rehabilitation.

The next face I saw was Floyd's. He brought me back to the present by asking, "Are you hurt?"

"I don't think so," I said. "Just shook up."

"It's ok, Kid. You're safe now. Don't go anywhere and, no matter what happens, don't say anything."

A few minutes later the foreman told me to go to the forge

office where I would be meeting with the plant safety committee. I walked into the office where the hammer crew had gathered after closing the steam valve.

My dad was also there. The stern look on his face told me that I was in real trouble. But rather than speaking to me he just shook his head and remained stone-faced during the entire proceeding. I didn't know, until then, the meaning of 'kangaroo court'.

The entire crew, except for Floyd, accused me of causing the accident. They said that as I pulled out, I stopped the forklift for an instant then, started back again. That caused the top die to slide off and drop toward the floor at the back of the hammer. It hit the treadle, releasing the ram to drop under a full head of steam, blowing out the gland, causing the steam to release through the gland toward the floor.

Each crew member gave his account and most of them said the same thing. "The forklift driver caused the accident."

But when Floyd gave his account of the incident, he detailed the series of events that caused the accident from a different perspective. He said that the crew had taken shortcuts to save time.

The seam valve was still fully open when it should have been closed. The ram should have had a two-by-four wedged between it and the anvil to prevent it from dropping accidentally. The die set should have had emery paper between the top and bottom halves to prevent the top half from sliding off.

He went on to say, "The die did not hit the treadle to cause the ram strike. The ram struck while the die was still falling. I think someone, in a rush to get out of the way, stepped on the treadle. None of this was the forklift driver's fault."

Nevertheless, the safety committee told me that they were going to write me up for violating forklift safety protocols.

In my mind, I was the accused in a court of law. The judge

announced the verdict: You have been tried and convicted of involuntary hammer slaughter. You are hereby sentenced to life in the drop-forge with no possibility of retirement."

"Don't bother writing me up," I told the Safety Committee. "This is my last day. I quit." I looked at my dad. He just shook his head once more, his face still stern, as I walked out of the office.

I left the drop-forge and never returned.

EPILOGUE

I never returned to college, but I have had several work experiences since then. I sold cars, founded and managed a successful retail store selling and servicing bicycles, became a partner in a small advertising agency, taught adult education classes, worked as a customer service representative for a credit card company, and was hired as an Employment and Training Specialist for the Wisconsin Department of Workforce Development where I was the business services representative.

After I retired, I launched a new career as a novelist, where I completed and published three novels. I am currently working on a fourth.

I have profound respect for the hard-working men and women in the manufacturing industry. They perform their jobs under very difficult conditions, showing up every day to produce the materials that are so important to every one of us.
And, although I consider my employment in the drop forge as my worst job ever, I learned several invaluable lessons that impacted my life afterward. I cannot help but admire and hold in the highest esteem, every one of the men with whom I worked. Blue-collar workers in industry and the farmers who provide our food are the foundation upon which our country is built.

Hats off to you, guys. And above all, stay safe.

ABOUT THE AUTHOR

J Frank Sander

 J Frank Sander has published three novels and numerous short stories on Amazon Kindle, and over fifty Op-ed's for the Milwaukee County Examiner website. He was a top prize winner in the Milwaukee Journal Wordsmith Contest for his memoir, Rubber Leg. He has written feature stories for publications such as Outside Magazine, the Racine Journal Times, the Milwaukee Journal, and others. A masterful storyteller, he draws from over seven decades of personal experiences for much of his fiction. Writing as Frank Tamel, he has authored three self-help books for people who are seeking employment. His primary interests include camping, fishing, dogs, firearms, and current events. He has four grown children and seven grandchildren. He lives in Wisconsin with his wife and three dogs.